Walking with Rainbows

by

Isla Dewar

First published in 2003 in Great Britain by
Barrington Stoke Ltd
www.barringtonstoke.co.uk

Reprinted 2005

ISBN 1-842991-30-2

Printed in Great Britain by Bell & Bain Ltd

A Note from the Author

When I was at school we had two kinds of heroes and heroines – classroom and playground. Those who did well inside school were not the ones who led the games and gossip outside in the playground.

Not that the classroom kids were teachers' pets. They were just people who could work that particular system. They did their schoolwork well and always handed in their homework on time. The playground kids, on the other hand, did do their homework, but only sometimes. They weren't bullies. They were, however, always popular with the other pupils. But not with the teachers.

Once, a boy who was a classroom kid did something stupid in one of our lessons. And the teacher said, "Simon, you were the boy the teachers in the staffroom voted most likely to succeed when you left school. How could you be so silly?" The whole class was stunned. Simon? We hardly noticed him. We had all thought Stephen, who played football, who all the girls fancied, far more likely to succeed out there in grown-up land. He was a bright, sunny, carefree character who knew all sorts of stuff they didn't teach in the classroom. That's what made me think about Briggsy. Someone who shines outside the system.

For Bob, Nick and Adam

Contents

Chapter 1

Briggsy

I'll never forget Briggsy. He was the most special friend a girl could ever have. At first I ignored him. I thought he was a bit thick. But he wasn't. He knew all sorts of stuff I didn't know. He told me about the stars and planets, how to find the Great Bear and Mars and Venus. He taught me how to make a pancake. He really did! He showed me how to play poker. How to dance. I never danced much, till I met Briggsy. He told me just to let go and do it. Hear the music. Let it get inside you. *Be* the music.

He wore bright colours. His T-shirts were red or green or orange. He hardly ever just walked anywhere, he'd do little dances, or skip ahead then walk backwards looking at me. He'd catch my eye and sing bits of songs he'd heard on the radio. He could do that, snapping his fingers and swaying with the music in his head, or pretending to play guitar. If I tried it, I looked silly, clumsy. He told me jokes that made me laugh. But mostly it's colours I think of when I remember him. Bright red trainers with no socks. Black jeans and those vivid T-shirts.

Stepping out with Briggsy was like walking with rainbows.

The year I met Briggsy the fair came to town early. It usually appeared in the middle of June just before the tourists turned up in busloads to walk along the harbour or spend time on the beach making sand castles, paddling in the sea, doing all the things people do when they're on holiday.

2

I never once saw the fair arriving. I'd get up one morning, and there it would be at the end of the harbour, all colours and lights and noise. It seemed to come from nowhere.

There was a big dipper and stalls selling hot dogs, burgers and candy floss. There was a carousel that played soft jingle-jangle music as huge painted wooden horses, unicorns and lions went round and round, up and down. There was a bingo stall, a small games arcade and dodgems. They were my favourite.

At the end of August, the fair people would take it all down. They must have worked all night, because I would wake one morning, and it would be gone. Just like that. The harbour would be grey and quiet and beyond it the sea would stretch for miles and miles. And someone arriving in our town on the morning the fair went away would never have known it had been there.

The first Monday in April Briggsy turned up in my class at school. He was two years older than anyone else, but had been put with us because he was behind in everything. I remember he was wearing a purple T-shirt. The headmaster had said that, as he was only going to be at school for one term while the fair was in town, he didn't have to buy a uniform. So there we all were in black jackets, and him sort of shining among us. At assembly he didn't just stick out. He glowed.

His family had the dodgems at the fair, and they moved about all over the country. Briggsy had never stayed anywhere long enough to go to school properly.

He had "a lot of catching up to do", our teacher Mrs Jackson told him. He would have to work hard. I remember how he nodded, saying he would in such a way that everyone, including Mrs Jackson, knew he wouldn't.

I'm spoilt. Everyone says so. Even Briggsy told me I was. "Minnie Grant, you're pampered," he said. "You think the world owes you something just 'cos you're in it."

Then he shook his head and said, "That ain't
the way it works." I stomped off in a huff.
I was mad at him for saying that. Because I
knew it was true.

I was born with a hole in my heart. It's
fine now. I'm fine now. But there was a time
when I was very, very little when my mum
and dad thought I might die. There are
pictures of me in the family photo album.
I'm tiny, really, really tiny. And I'm in this
plastic incubator. There are tubes sticking
into me, and they're attached to all sorts of
machines. But I'm lying there with thin,
stick-like arms waving in the air.

My mum says this was so like me. There I
was, lying screaming my head off and waving
my arms about, when everyone was beating
themselves up thinking I was about to die.

Well, I'm still here. I had some operations
that I don't really remember. I got better.
But as far as my parents are concerned, I'm
frail and delicate. I need to be kept safe and

warm. When I was a kid, I was never allowed out to play with other kids. At the first sign of winter, I was wrapped up in scarves, gloves and this horrible green woolly hat. No-one else wore a hat.

I was given anything I wanted. Even now, anything I ask for I get. Clothes, shoes, CDs, a mobile phone, the lot. Briggsy said I didn't know most people had to work to get those things, *earn* them.

My mum pampers me. She worries that I might get ill. At night, when my mates are allowed out to the cinema or to parties, I have to be home by nine o'clock. I hate this. When I was little Mum used to walk me to school. Long after everyone else was turning up on their own, she was leaving me at the gate with a little kiss, and me in that horrible green hat. Mothers can make you cringe.

I have a feeling that mothers can go on embarrassing you all your life. My sister is ten years older than me. She's married. But when she first brought her boyfriend Robbie home, my mum told him, "Our Sue was a terrible little girl. She sucked her thumb till she was ten, and she was always picking her nose."

Sue shouted, "MUM! Stop telling him that!"

But Mum carried right on, telling him all about the naughty, silly things Sue did when she was little. Like the time she cut off her hair with the scissors she'd nicked from the kitchen drawer. Then there was the time she said she was going to run away. When nobody could find her, Mum thought she really had gone off. She got into such a state, she was going to call the police. Only Dad came home from work and found Sue in the cupboard in the hall eating a packet of chocolate biscuits.

Sue hid her face in her hands when Mum told these stories. But Robbie reached out and put his arm round her. "I just love hearing all about you," he'd said. "Tell me more."

And he'd looked at Sue. His eyes all gentle and warm. I could see he loved her. Whatever she'd done, he loved her. I thought, *that's what I want one day, somebody who'll look at me like that.*

Chapter 2
Joey Classes

In our school we call them "joey" classes. Other schools have different names. But in our school joey classes are for the joeys. I'm a joey at maths. That means I'm rubbish when it comes to adding, subtracting and all that stuff. Briggsy was in the joey class for everything. Not that he cared. Marc, my boyfriend, wasn't in any joey classes at all. He was good at everything. I could hate him for that.

I really got to know Briggsy in detention. Me and Marc and Briggsy were always there.

Me because I was always saying things I didn't really mean. Like asking teachers why I had to do maths when I was no good at it, and telling them I wasn't going to do anything needing maths when I grew up. Then I would sit at my desk with my arms folded and refuse to do any work. Briggsy got detention because he never did anything in class except draw in his school books. And Marc got it because he was sulky and never did anything anyone asked him to.

Marc and me had been going out together for months. He was in the year above me. He was tall with dark hair and he was good-looking in a moody sort of way. He used to be rich. But now he isn't. Something to do with his dad putting money into a business that failed, or something. He used to have a swimming pool and everything. Now he lives in a house that's the same as mine. Ordinary. Just a house with a bit of garden at the front and a bigger bit at the back.

Marc never said much. He was the strong silent type, I used to think. But now I've decided he was just missing his old life. He'd gone to a private school. Lived in a big house. Had designer clothes. Now he was just like the rest of us. Walking along ordinary streets, wearing ordinary shoes. Like me. I guessed it must be hard.

Detention was at lunchtime. We had to eat our lunch in ten minutes, and then from one to half-past we had to work. Marc, who was good at everything, used the time to do his homework. I did maths. Badly.

Briggsy didn't do anything. He just sat drumming his fingers and jiggling in his seat to some song that was playing in his head.

"Haven't you got work to do, Mr Briggs?" said Miss Brown, the science teacher, who was taking detention that day.

"I've got lots of work to do, Miss," said Briggsy. "I'm doing it. Right now."

"You seem to be drumming your fingers and wriggling," said Miss Brown.

"That's how it may seem to you," said Briggsy. "But I'm thinking about the work I have to do. Planning it. Getting it straight in my head."

Miss Brown glared at him over the top of her glasses. And Briggsy continued to drum his fingers and jiggle about. I sniggered. A sort of snorting sound that came from my nose. I wish I didn't do that.

"Is something amusing you, Minnie?" Miss Brown asked.

"No," I told her. I acted all innocent. And then she asked why I was in detention.

"Cheek," I told her.

"Then today's detention doesn't seem to have helped you," she said. "You'll do detention for the rest of the week till you've learnt your lesson."

12

"That's not fair," I shouted. "I only snorted."

"You want to be kept in next week as well?" she asked.

I shook my head and shut up. From his desk Briggsy smiled at me and shrugged. I think he was saying sorry. When it was time to go to our classes, he caught up with me as we left the room. "Can I take you for a coffee after school?" he asked.

I said, "Only if Marc can come too."

He said, "Sure. No problem."

That's how we all got together. And going down the High Street after school became a routine.

First we'd hit Boots. I liked to check out the shampoos. I have a thing about shampoo. It has to be right. There's de-gunking shampoo. And shampoo to give you volume. And shampoo to make your hair shiny.

I always think you can't have enough shampoo.

If you use the same shampoo all the time, it stops working. That's what I think, anyway. So I always have lots of different ones.

Then we'd look at the lipsticks and nail varnish. When I'd used up all my nails trying out different shades, Briggsy would let me use his. Marc hated this. He'd tut and sigh, and blow out his cheeks. He thought all this stuff too girly.

After that it was Woolworths. We'd flick through the CDs, picking which one we'd buy next. We'd look at the magazines. Or maybe the cards and pick out the rude ones.

Then it was down to Bob's caff for cappuccinos, with lots of chocolate sprinkled on top.

We'd sit in the window and watch the people passing by. I always had a frothy moustache on my upper lip.

14

Briggsy knew all about people. He watched how they moved, how they walked. He looked at their expressions. Me? I just looked at their clothes. And I only had two descriptions for them. They were either brilliant or naff.

Still, we decided two things:

1. Old ladies with mobile phones look really funny.

2. Old men often have no bums.

I don't know where old men's bums go to. But as men get older their bums really do seem to fade away.

Mostly what we did was giggle. I don't think I ever had as much fun with anyone as I did with Briggsy.

And always, always, at quarter to five, Briggsy would get up, take his bag and say, "Got to get going."

"Where are you going?" I asked.

"Home," he said. "Got to cook for the folks."

Chapter 3

Cooking and Singing

Things I hate. Though maybe not in this order:

1. Wasps.

2. People who talk about me to someone else when I'm standing there, too. Like when I was in the supermarket with Mum and she met Mrs Pratt. She isn't really Mrs Pratt. She's Mrs Platt. But I call her Mrs Pratt 'cos I don't like her. Anyway, Mrs Pratt said to Mum, "Is that your Minnie? I hardly knew her. Hasn't she grown?"

She was talking to my mum about me as if I wasn't there. And of course I'd grown. I'm a teenager. It's what I do. Grow.

3. Hearing my heart beat.

I hate it when I'm awake in the middle of the night, and the whole house is silent. Everything's black. There are creaks and clicks but they don't frighten me, because they're the noises the house makes when nobody's moving about in it.

But my head's against the pillow. And in that pillow ear I can hear my heart. It's a soft squishy sound. *Boop, boop, boop.* I hate hearing it, I'm scared it'll stop.

I told Briggsy about how I hated to hear my heart beating.

He said, "Don't be daft. If it stopped, you wouldn't hear it. You'd be dead."

"But," I said, "there might be a moment. The shortest moment between my heart stopping and me popping off. When I'd know the beating was gone, and I was going to die."

He looked at me and said, "That won't happen." Then, "Don't worry. Everybody has fears like that."

"Do they?" I said. "I thought it was only me."

Sometimes I think about being me. I stop and I think, *I'm really me.*

It was like singing. Not that I can sing. Not that I think I am like a song or anything like that. But when I sing, it sounds lovely to me. What I hear inside me is not what other people hear. Outside in the world my singing sounds awful.

"Please, Minnie," Mum would say. "I'm trying to think."

"Pack it in, Min," Marc would say. "You're doing my head in."

So I'd stop singing even though it didn't sound that bad to me inside.

I have the same problem just being me. Like, for example, I was walking along the corridor, thinking about nothing really. Not happy. Not sad. Somewhere between the two. Then Mrs Jackson passed me and said, "Cheer up, Minnie. It may never happen."

What may never happen? I wasn't worrying about anything. I was just walking along.

It must be my face, I thought. I have the sort of face that has a sad and sulky look when I'm not doing anything with it.

Then I have these moments. I call them my *reality moments*. The ones when I'm me. I'm walking along the street, or I'm sitting in a classroom, or I'm standing in the playground and I suddenly think, *Gosh, I'm me. This is me. I'm real.*

And everything about me suddenly seems real. More than real. Sort of really real. The noises are louder. And I don't hear what someone is saying to me because I'm looking at them and thinking they are *real*, and I watch them and the way their lips move. It all seems daft.

I told Briggsy about this *being real* thing.

He said, "Yeah. Everybody has moments like that."

"Do they?" I said. "I thought it was only me."

"Nah," he said. "It's not just you. Your reality moments aren't what make you special. Everyone's special in one way or another. You're special just 'cos you're you. Come over to my place on Saturday. I'll cook you a meal, 'cos you're special."

This cooking thing had got to me and Marc a bit. Marc thought Briggsy a bit soft because he let me put varnish on his nails, and because he was in the joey class for everything, and because he cooked.

"Briggsy, men don't cook," I said.

"Of course men cook," he said. "Loads of men cook. Jamie Oliver and that. Men are the best cooks."

Briggsy beat his chest like Tarzan and made me laugh. Briggsy was always making me laugh.

Chapter 4
Looking for Stars

I went to Briggsy's for supper that Saturday. Marc was away at a wedding. His cousin was getting married.

We had to eat early. He had two little sisters who got hungry. So I went down to the fairground just before five.

Briggsy lived in a mobile home parked behind the fair. It was amazing. Everything was so easy to reach. It was really neat. It had three rooms. A bedroom for his sisters and a bedroom for Briggsy's mum and dad.

Briggsy slept on the sofa bed in the living room. It had the biggest telly I'd ever seen.

And as I looked around the living room, I realised Briggsy could lie in his bed every night watching telly. Cool.

I thought this was *so* cool that the next day I said to Mum that if we sold the house, we could buy a huge mobile home and go wherever we wanted.

She just looked at me. One of those looks only mums can do. The look that makes you think you're really stupid and not worth bothering with.

"Go and wash your hands," she said. "It's suppertime."

"I take it," I said, "that you're not going to get a mobile home, then?"

Mum was mashing potatoes. She stopped, looked at me and said, "No, we're not."

So I never mentioned it again.

But back to Briggsy and the meal. He made me a spicy chicken dish. It was little strips of chicken in some crispy batter stuff, with rice that was also hot and spicy and that had peas in it. And there was salad, too. It was the most fantastic thing I'd ever eaten.

"Where did you learn to cook?" I asked.

Briggsy waved his hand at the telly. "I was watching *Ready, Steady, Cook*. And I thought, *that looks easy. I could do that*. So I did."

Of course, at first he'd made a real mess in the kitchen. Pots, pans everywhere. And everything burnt black. But, slowly, he'd got the hang of it.

It crossed my mind that Briggsy knew a lot of stuff he hadn't picked up at school. He was cleverer than anyone thought.

After we'd eaten we went out to the fair. I wanted to go to the fruit machines. On

Saturdays I got my pocket money. I thought I could use it to make more money. I have a thing about money. I want lots of it. I'd like to have a fortune so I could buy anything I want.

Like I'll be looking at a magazine and I'll see fantastic clothes and I think it would be great to just go and buy them. Or I'll see a room with amazing sofas, and I think, *that'd do me*. If I had lots of money I could snap my fingers, and the sofas would be mine. At the same time I fancied getting hold of a pile of money so I could buy a mobile home. Like Briggsy's.

I lost all my pocket money on the fruit machines.

"These dumb machines have eaten all my cash," I said.

"Course they have," Briggsy told me. "What would be the point of them if they didn't take your money?"

"What do you mean?" I asked.

"People take them all over the country, set them up. It's how they make their living. If you made money from them, they wouldn't."

I could see he was making sense. That was the last time I ever gambled.

Still, I got on the big dipper and the dodgems for free because Briggsy was with the fair. That was fantastic.

Then he walked me home. I was going along, head bent back, looking up. I'm always watching the sky at night, hoping to see shooting stars.

"You might see one," Briggsy told me. "But August is the time for shooting stars. That's when you get a whole load of them, showers of them. Whoosh."

"How do you know that?" I needed to know.

"Telly," he said. "*The Sky at Night*. Patrick Moore. He's a really cool guy."

Then he showed me the sky. Took me on a trip through the stars. He pointed out the Pole Star and the Milky Way and the Bear. He knew so much. You'd never think he was in the joey class for everything.

Chapter 5

Millionaires

Mum and Dad had gone out to the pub when we got back to my house. Briggsy came in for a coffee. We sat on the sofa and put on the telly.

Who Wants To Be A Millionaire was on. It was amazing, Briggsy could answer nearly all the questions.

"How do you know all that stuff?" I asked him. All the things he knew, that I didn't, sometimes it got to me.

He shrugged. "Telly. Quiz shows. *The Weakest Link* and that. And I pick up things watching programmes at night in my bed."

"You're wicked," I said. And I told him he should try to get on the show. He could be a millionaire. And give me a few thousand of my own for letting him use my mobile.

So we dialled the number. In fact, that night we dialled the number over 20 times. Then, over the next few weeks, we kept on trying.

We only stopped when the bill for my mobile came in. My dad always paid it for me, of course. This time he went ballistic. He stomped about all over the house waving it, shouting that it was over 300 pounds and it was usually only 20 pounds or so.

He looked at the list of calls. And, when he called the number we had dialled over and over again, he found out it was *Who Wants To Be A Millionaire*. He and Mum stopped my pocket money for a month to help pay the bill. I was told never to phone again and try to get Briggsy on the show.

I tried to explain that if Briggsy won, and he surely would because he knew so much, I'd get a cut so the phone bill would easily be paid.

I told my mum and dad that if there was a question about soaps, which Briggsy never watched, he would have to ask the audience. But he was very good on animals because of all the wildlife programmes he'd seen.

"Even if he only wins 250,000 pounds, he's going to give me 50,000. That would pay the phone bill for months," I said.

I was imagining all the shoes and CDs I could buy. "And I could get a mobile home for us," I said.

Mum said never to mention quiz shows or mobile homes again. Ever.

I stomped out. They just didn't understand.

As I left the room I heard my dad say, "She's spoilt."

My mum didn't say anything. But I knew she was nodding her head, agreeing with him.

Chapter 6

Boot Sales

Cross Farm is just on the edge of our town. In summer Mr Jack, who owns the farm, has car boot sales in one of his fields. It happens every second Sunday. People come from miles and miles around to set up stalls and sell stuff they no longer need. And even more people come to rummage through the piles of that stuff looking for bargains.

Briggsy wanted to go. But Marc and I didn't. We thought it was naff.

But Briggsy said, "You never know what you'll find. Maybe something worth a quid or two."

"No way," said Marc.

"Yeah," said Briggsy. "People don't know what they have. It could be an old vase or a set of cups that was handed down when their granny died. They think it's horrible and want to get rid of it. But it's worth a fortune." And he jumped and punched the air as if he'd scored in the World Cup final. "An absolute fortune," he shouted again.

Marc and me looked at him like he was daft. But come Sunday, we went with him to the boot sale. It was hard to say no to Briggsy. He made everything sound like fun, and you kind of got swept along. Besides, I was interested in making a fortune.

The boot sale was, as expected, naff. Well, that's what me and Marc thought, anyway.

Briggsy said, "Wow. This is great." And he went off to poke about and see what he could find.

It was mostly rubbish as far as I could see. People were standing around with their things spread out on tables. There were people selling old records, and people selling piles of junk like spoons and forks and worn-out shoes. And people selling rubbish clothes. It all looked like masses and masses of things most people would put in the bin.

But I bought a red T-shirt that dyed everything in the wash. And two CDs, one of which didn't play properly. Marc bought some comics.

Briggsy bought three plates.

"Plates?" I said.

"Yeah, plates," Briggsy replied.

They seemed old and had a sort of cracked look about them.

"What do you want them for?" I asked.

"I'm going to sell 'em," he grinned.

So we walked back into town, to the High Street. We stopped at The Captain's Antiques Shop. Briggsy took the plates in while me and Marc hung about outside. Ten minutes later Briggsy came out waving a tenner. He'd bought the plates for 50 pence. What a profit!

"How come you knew the plates were worth something?" I asked Briggsy.

He shrugged. "*Antiques Roadshow.* Watch it every week."

I stood there holding the T-shirt I'd bought. My hands were red from the dye that had come off it. And I had my CDs. One looked really damaged and dodgy when I looked at it closely. I thought how life was one long reality moment for Briggsy. His teachers thought he was behind in all his subjects because he hadn't stayed anywhere long enough to learn the things they taught in school. But outside of school, Briggsy was way ahead of everybody. He knew loads of things.

He was good at life. Marc and me with our comics and our cheap rubbish were the joeys at that.

Chapter 7

Things I Love

I wrote a list of things I love best in the world. I wrote them in this book Marc gave me for Christmas. It's a lovely notebook. It has thick glossy blue covers with *Notes* in gold letters. I write all my secret things in it. Like wishes – I wish I lived in a mobile home, like Briggsy. I wish Marc wasn't so sulky. I wish I had long legs and thick eyelashes. That sort of thing.

My list of things I like best

1. *Maltesers*

2. Walking along the street with Briggsy. And him making me laugh.

3. My mum's homemade chocolate cake

4. Shooting stars

My list went on like that. I wanted to write that I secretly loved Marc, but I was afraid someone might read it. Also I thought that if I wrote it down, everything might fall apart. Marc would stop seeing me. So I kept it a secret inside my head.

On the Friday after the boot sale school broke up for summer. We had weeks and weeks of doing nothing. I was looking forward to it. Staying in bed late in the morning. Watching afternoon films on telly. Hanging about the caff drinking cappuccino or coke. Or just lying in the back garden trying to get a tan. I had it all planned.

It was the best summer ever. I saw Marc every day. We went to the fair and, if it wasn't busy, we got free rides on the dodgems from Briggsy. He'd stand on the bumper at the back, and we'd whoosh around, banging into people. All the time music played, and lights glittered. I was really happy.

In the afternoon we lay on the beach, out beside the cliffs. We swam, though the water was cold. We ducked under the waves, and splashed each other.

At night, when I was in bed, Marc would phone me. Once when I said I was lying with my head on the pillow talking to him, he said, "Lucky pillow." I thought, *cool.*

The days drifted by. And music seemed to play in my head all the time. My mum and dad started giving me pocket money again. They stopped going on about the huge phone bill. I never phoned to get Briggsy on *Who Wants To Be A Millionaire* again. I had a new way to make a fortune – antiques. I had a plan. We would find things at the boot sale, and sell them to the antiques shop and make a fortune. We would buy a mobile home, me and Marc and Briggsy. We'd set off, and just go wherever we wanted. We'd be happy.

We went to the boot sale every time it was on. I never did find anything worth a fortune. Neither did Marc. But Briggsy found things – a record that he took to the dealer's stall and sold for five pounds when he'd paid 50 pence for it, a chair he carried all the way back into town and got 25 pounds for. He knew what he was doing. I didn't. I saw my dream slipping away.

Still, the summer was magic.

At the beginning of August, Marc went on holiday to visit his aunt in Cornwall, with his whole family. Briggsy was working every day at the fair. I wandered about, looking at lipsticks, clicking through CDs in Woolworths, alone. Sometimes, after tea, I went down to the fair to listen to the music, to watch the people and to feel the fun, the buzz of things going on. Sometimes I'd go to the railway bridge and watch the trains. I loved doing that. I loved dreaming of all the places the trains were going.

That's the thing about living in a small place. The young people all talk about leaving. You dream about the rest of the world. The things going on. Yellow taxis in New York streets, clubs in London. All the stuff you can do. When here in this tiny town, there is nothing going on at all. The only bright light is a small caff that sells cappuccino.

One day, about a week before school went back, Briggsy took me aside. The fair was playing, there was the smell of burgers, people were laughing, I could hardly hear what he said.

"Still want to see shooting stars?"

"Yes!" I told him.

"Tomorrow night there's a big storm of shooting stars passing."

"Excellent," I said.

"You want to watch them? I'll meet up with you just after two. And we'll go out to the cliffs and you'll see a thousand stars going over."

"Two?" I said. "Not in the afternoon, I suppose?"

"No, Minnie. Two in the morning. I'll meet you here by the dodgems."

Chapter 8
Shooting Stars

I had never been out late at night. Not on my own, anyway. But I wanted to see the shooting stars. So that night I lay in bed telling myself not to fall asleep. Just before two, I got up and pulled on my jeans and a T-shirt. I sneaked down the hall, to check that Mum and Dad were sleeping. They were, I could hear them snoring. Then I climbed out of my bedroom window and went to meet Briggsy.

It wasn't cold. The air was warm and soft. It was so quiet, not a soul about. I could hear

my footsteps on the pavement as I walked.
It's funny, everything you know well, streets,
houses that you pass every day, look different
at night. I was a little scared. I kept looking
back making sure nobody was following me.
And sometimes I tiptoed so that anybody who
might follow me wouldn't hear me. Daft.

Briggsy was waiting for me at the edge of
the fairground. It was silent at this time of
night. In the dark the dodgems and the big
dipper looked a different shape. They looked
large and scary. I thought that if I was a
ghost, I'd haunt an empty fairground at night.

We walked along past the houses that
faced the shore. As we passed the Old Ship
Inn, we could hear voices and laughter coming
from inside.

"A lock-in," said Briggsy.

"A what?" I said.

"Girl, you know nothing. After closing
time, they pull the curtains, and lock the

doors so you think the pub's shut. But inside the lights are on, and everyone just keeps on drinking and having a good time. A lock-in."

"Right. So what we're having is a lock-out. When I'm supposed to be home in bed tucked up. But I'm out here having a good time."

"Excellent," he said.

We walked on. After the last house there was a grass track that led to the foot of the cliffs. Then there were old wooden steps to the top. Two hundred steps. It's a long climb, but there's a rusty iron rail to hold on to. Briggsy ran up the steps, two at a time. I came along behind him, slowly. Puffing and panting. Every now and then I'd stop to look up at the sky, in case shooting stars were happening already and I was missing them.

When I reached the top, Briggsy was there already, jumping about, excited. It wasn't dark that night. There was a huge potato moon.

"A potato moon," I said to Briggsy. "The moon's not quite full, so it's all lumpy like a potato."

"We could make moon chips," he said. "Moon chips and fish with salt and vinegar."

"Mashed moon and sausages," I giggled.

I shivered. I rubbed my arms, which had goose bumps from the cold. It might have been soft and warm down in my street, outside my bedroom window but up here on the top of the cliffs it was windy. And cold. I was all hot and sweaty from the long climb. I just knew I was getting a chill. My mum would ask how I got it. And I'd say, "Dunno."

And then I saw it. It flashed across the sky, with a long trailing tail. *Whoosh*, a shooting star. I jumped about, pointing up. "There's one. There's one."

Briggsy saw it. We both stood, heads bent back, watching. Then there was another, skimming over the sky.

48

We watched it fade away. After that – nothing.

I felt the wind cutting through me. I started to shiver.

"That's it, then," I said. "We should go home now."

Briggsy said, "That's never it. That's just the beginning. There'll be thousands of them along soon."

I couldn't miss that. So I stayed even though my teeth were chattering. I was freezing.

Every now and then another star would appear whizzing far above us. And we would watch it in wonder. But by about four o'clock I was seriously cold and wishing I was in bed. It was getting light, the sky was turning pale.

And then they came. Hundreds of them, shooting over us. They were flying out of the darkness. A huge shower of stars with tails trailing behind them. I'd never seen anything like it. I forgot how cold I was and started to run about, shouting.

"Fantastic, fantastic."

Briggsy was shouting too. "Like fireworks."

It *was* like fireworks. Only better, they were real. I was standing under a huge, moving sparkle. "Wow! Great!"

"Like rockets," Briggsy said. "Real rockets."

"Rockets rocketing over the sky."

Then they were gone. Now there were only ordinary stars in the ordinary sky. I was sad. Really sad. They say that if you see a shooting star you get a wish. And I'd had hundreds of wishes passing over me, and I hadn't asked for anything.

"I forgot to make a wish," I said.

Briggsy said, "Can't you just think it was fantastic? It isn't about wishes. It's about just seeing them and feeling glad."

I suppose he was right. Still, I wished I'd wished for a mobile home. Sometimes when I'm making wishes, I just wish for something wonderful to happen. I hadn't even done that.

We walked home. The first birds were singing. It was almost five o'clock, and still everything was quiet. The streets were empty, all the curtains in all the houses were drawn.

I thought about the people in them, sleeping cosily under their duvets, snoring while thousands of shooting stars flew over their rooftops. They'd missed it.

And that made me glad I'd seen it. I was suddenly so happy. When we reached the end of my street, I flung my arms round Briggsy's neck and kissed him.

"Thanks. Thanks for everything."

"It's OK," he said.

He turned and walked away. I was still shaking with cold, but I watched till he had gone. Briggsy seemed just to fade into the new morning.

Chapter 9

The Last Boot Sale

I climbed back through my bedroom window. I couldn't get back into bed quick enough. My feet were wet, I hadn't noticed. I had never been so cold in my life. The chill seemed to go down into my bones. I lay under my duvet shivering, and thinking about shooting stars.

Next day I felt weird. I couldn't eat. When I wasn't trembling with cold, I was coming out in horrible sweats. I stayed in bed till about one o'clock, then I got up.

I wanted to go to the boot sale. It was the last one of the year. My last chance to find something really valuable and make my fortune.

I met Briggsy and Marc at the fairground, where we always met on boot sale days. I was really pleased to see Marc now he was back from his holidays. But he was being all funny because I'd been out late at night with Briggsy. I thought he was jealous because we'd seen the shooting stars and he hadn't. That was a bit over the top.

I could hardly walk out to the field. The strange thing is when you feel dizzy and your knees go all wobbly you never think you're ill. You just think, *Ooh, I feel ever so funny.* I could hardly breathe and I had a horrible pain in my chest. I was sweating loads.

Marc was quite nice about how long it was taking to get to the boot sale. But Briggsy, who always said you had to get there early to get the good stuff, was grumpy. In the end he ran on ahead, saying he'd meet us there.

He must have been at the sale for about a quarter of an hour before Marc and I arrived. I was feeling really wobbly now and my legs could hardly hold me up. I was drenched in sweat. I felt awful.

We saw Briggsy by a table that a young couple had set up. He was watching as someone bought a small statue thing. I couldn't see it properly. It looked like a pig. It wasn't very nice. I'd never have bought it.

The man buying the horrible little pig thing was saying, "Nah, mate. It's a fake. I'll give you a fiver for it."

And the couple selling the horrible pig thing said, "OK, then."

Briggsy was pretending he wasn't interested. He was picking up plates and cups, turning them over, then putting them back.

Then I couldn't believe what I was seeing.

The man buying the pig put it down as he got his wallet out of his pocket. And Briggsy put his hand over the pig, gently lifted it up and walked away. It was all so fast, and sort of easy, it was as if it wasn't happening.

Briggsy put the little china pig thing into his pocket, then just melted into the crowd. I saw him a few seconds later, at another stall. After that I lost sight of him again.

By now Marc and me were close enough to the man who'd been buying the pig to hear what was going on.

The man shouted, "Hey! That lad's taken my china pig."

And the man selling the pig said, "I didn't see anything."

The pig buyer said, "Well it's been nicked. I think we should call the police."

The pig seller said, "Hardly worth calling the police over a five pound fake."

And the pig buyer said, "That was no fake. That was Chinese, probably about 600 years old. It was worth a bomb."

And the pig seller went a funny colour. It was hard to tell who he was madder at, the bloke for trying to buy it for a fiver, or Briggsy for stealing it.

I was going a funny colour myself. A sort of greeny-white. Sweat was running down my back. I felt all faint and floppy. I had to sit down, I couldn't stand up any more. I just sank to the ground.

And as I sat on the mud with people walking past looking down at me, I saw Briggsy by the entrance of the field. There were lots of people there, and he just seemed to mix in with them. Then he was gone. He just seemed to fade away.

Chapter 10

Dreams

I don't know how I got home. I remember walking back along the road with Marc. Well, leaning on Marc, really. I had a horrible pain in my chest. It hurt to breathe. I counted steps. One step nearer my house. Two steps nearer. And all the time I was thinking that Briggsy was a thief.

When we arrived at my front door, Marc rang the bell. My mother answered. I think I fell into her arms.

She got me upstairs and into bed. After that all I remember is dreams.

I was in a sort of coma. I felt as if I was floating far away from everybody. I know the doctor came, because afterwards my mum told me he had. I was given an injection and all sorts of pills. And for a while my mum, dad and the doctor thought they'd have to move me to hospital.

Though I didn't know about any of this. Because I was ill. I was lying in bed, sweating and dreaming. I dreamed about stars and mud. I dreamed that I woke up one morning and my room was empty. All my things, my CD-player and all my CDs, my clothes, everything had been stolen. I hated that dream.

The worst thing about nightmares is you can't stop them. You just lie there in bed and they come at you. If a nightmare was a horrible film on the telly you could just reach for the remote control and switch it off.

Mum told me later I'd been shouting things out. "I don't know what you were on about. Things about moon chips and fish. And shooting stars."

It seems the chill I'd got when I was out with Briggsy on the cliff looking for shooting stars had spread through me. Every bit of my insides had caught it. Even my kidneys. They had stopped working properly. This is not good when you already have a wonky heart.

I was out of it for about three days. And even after I was sitting up in bed and well enough to eat a little soup, my mum wouldn't let anyone in to see me.

So it was over a week before I found out what had happened.

Marc came by and at last Mum said, "All right, you can go and say hello. But don't stay long."

Marc sat on my bed and told me all the things that had happened while I had been sweating and dreaming in my bed.

Chapter 11
What Briggsy Did

Briggsy *had* stolen the horrible china piggy. He'd been standing at a table looking at the things for sale, and had seen it. As he was reaching for it, a man took it and turned it over in his hands, looking at it.

Briggsy knew it was worth lots, and had hoped the man would put it down. But he didn't. He'd offered the couple selling it a fiver.

Briggsy watched. He knew the man trying to buy the pig was a dealer and was about to make a pile of money selling it. And he knew the couple selling the china pig were broke.

Briggsy could tell about people. He knew from the way they stood, or held their shoulders, or bent their heads, if they were feeling down or feeling happy. He could watch couples in the caff where we had coffee and say if they were on their first date or if they'd been seeing each other for ages. It was in the way they looked at one another, or spoke, or fiddled with their spoons. I thought he was amazing.

I suppose Briggsy felt sorry for the people selling the china pig. That's why he stole it before the dealer had paid for it. That way, because the money hadn't been handed over, it still belonged to the couple.

After that he slipped out of the boot sale, and ran all the way back to town. He went to the antique shop. There he sold the china pig for 500 pounds.

"Five hundred quid," I said. "Wow. That's loads. That would have been the start of my fortune."

"Shut up about your fortune, Minnie," said Marc.

"Was Briggsy chuffed with himself?" I asked. "Did he buy anything with the money?" I needed to know.

Marc shook his head. "Nah."

Marc had taken me home that Sunday. Then he'd gone to find Briggsy. It wasn't hard to guess where he might be. Marc went to the antique shop, and met Briggsy coming out looking very pleased with himself.

"Made yourself a fortune?" Marc asked.

"I did very nicely," Briggsy told him. Then he set off tanking up the street.

Marc had to run to catch up with him. "Where are you going?"

"Back to the boot sale," Briggsy told him.

"Haven't you made enough for one day?"

And Briggsy turned to him. "This isn't for me. That dealer was about to rip off the people selling the pig. I nicked it, so he wouldn't. Now I've got to get back to give them the money before they leave."

The pair of them ran back to the field. They got there just as everyone was packing up to go home.

Briggsy found the couple who'd been selling the pig and, before they could say anything, he handed them the money. "There, mate," he said. "You should check the value of your things before you sell them off cheap at boot sales."

I wanted to know what the man had said. How had he looked? Was he gobsmacked?

But Marc said he didn't know. Right then, the dealer who'd been trying to buy the pig for a fiver turned up. He wasn't very pleased. In fact, he was furious. And he had a couple of friends with him. "Big friends," said Marc. "Big, beefy friends."

Briggsy had taken one look at them, and legged it. He took off at top speed. There had been a lot of people leaving, a big crowd at the gate of the field.

"Briggsy just melted into them," Marc went on. "He disappeared. Just like that. I never saw him again."

Marc had looked and looked. But Briggsy was gone.

Next day school started for the new term. Briggsy wasn't there.

All the tourists had gone home. And the fair had been taken down overnight. It was gone, too.

So Marc didn't know what the couple thought when Briggsy gave them the money.

But I like to imagine the moment when they took hold of the cash. I like to think they were jumping around and hugging each other. I like to think they cried.

After that it was time for Marc to go. He leaned over and kissed me, ever so softly. And he said, "Take care of yourself, Minnie. See you soon."

It was as good as seeing shooting stars.

Chapter 12
More Stars

Next day I was allowed to get up. My legs were all wobbly. They felt like jelly. I didn't think they'd hold me up. But I went over to the window and looked out. The harbour was all grey again. A few little boats were bobbing about. But the fair wasn't there. No lights, no jangly music. It was as if it had never been there.

Somehow I knew I'd never see Briggsy again. And I didn't, though the fair came back the next summer, Briggsy and his family weren't with it.

But I did hear from him again. He sent me a letter. It came a week after Marc had come to see me. He'd come often after that. He brought me grapes and chocolate. We'd sit on the sofa after he'd finished school and we'd watch films on the telly. And we'd chat and snog a bit. He told me he'd been madly jealous when I went looking for shooting stars with Briggsy.

"There will be more shooting stars," I said. "You won't miss them."

"I'm not jealous of you seeing shooting stars. I'm jealous of Briggsy being alone out on the cliffs with you, at night."

And I said, "Oh." I hadn't thought of that. Sometimes I'm so thick.

Marc would tell me about school since I still wasn't well enough to go to it. I got all the gossip. And we'd chat about Briggsy,

remembering all the things he did. We'd
wonder where he was now. I missed Briggsy.

Then the letter came. It was written in
the scrawly way he wrote things down.

Hi Minnie,

How're you doing? Miss me? I
suppose you'll have heard all about me
selling the china pig and taking the money
to the people back at the boot sale.

Fun, eh?

I've sent you something to remind you
of me. I hope you wear it.

Listen, Min. This thing you have about
making a fortune, it's daff. You have
lots of things to be glad about. You have
a nice home. You're funny and good-
looking in a cheeky sort of way. And Marc
is nuts about you. He told me.

Seems to me if you have all that, you don't need a fortune.

I hope you go and have cappuccino every day. And when you do, think about me. I'll think about you, too.

Love,

Briggsy

There was a small packet inside the letter. I opened it up. It was a silver chain, and on it a cluster of stars, all joined together. It was lovely.

I showed it to Mum. "Look what Briggsy sent me."

"Oh, Minnie. It's beautiful." She helped me put it on, fastening it at the back of my neck.

I read the letter again and again. And Mum saw me wiping away a tear with the back of my hand.

"I miss Briggsy," I told her.

"Of course you do," she said.

I told her all about what he'd done. How he'd stolen the china pig and then sold it and taken the money to the young couple.

"That was brave of him."

"I thought he was a thief," I said.

"Maybe that's why you dreamed about all your precious things being stolen," Mum said. "Maybe you were thinking that if one important person was gone from you, all your things would go, too."

I was surprised. Mum was probably right. Sometimes mums can amaze you. You think they're thinking about what's for tea, and they come out with something that shows they understand exactly how you're feeling.

"Briggsy was like a rainbow," I said. "He wore all those bright colours. And he could sing and dance about and pretend to play the guitar and it seemed OK. If I did that, I'd look silly. And he knew all sorts of stuff, about cooking and antiques. And the stars."

I never did tell her how I got ill. I never mentioned going out late to look for shooting stars and getting chilled. She'd have been really mad at me. I kept it a secret.

"Briggsy knew all about the stars," I said. "He was all sorts of colours. When I was with him it was like walking with rainbows. Now he's gone. He's just faded away."

My mum touched my cheek. "That's what they do – fade away. Rainbows are like that. But you always remember them."

Chapter 13
More Lists

I made two more lists to help me sort things out in my head.

Things that make me miserable

1. I'll never see Briggsy again.

2. I haven't made a fortune.

But I thought I'd forget that second one for a while. I'd leave it till after I'd left school, and would really have the time to get down to it.

Things that make me glad

1. Marc and me are getting along just fine.

2. When I was ill, I lost weight – five whole pounds. Though I am putting it back on now I'm eating again.

3. I've seen shooting stars.

4. I had at least met Briggsy. He had made me laugh. He'd shown me all sorts of things I hadn't known about. I had been his friend, and being his friend was like walking with rainbows.

When I think about it, I know I'm really, really lucky to be me.

Barrington Stoke would like to thank all its readers for commenting on the manuscript before publication and in particular:

Ben Annable
Miles Bailey
Emily Branson
Lauren Breese
Chris Brown
Nick Bull
Karin Carter
Thomas Carter
Rachel Davis
L. Donnachie
K. Firth-Jones
A. Frampton
Chris Furniss
E. Harrison
Jamie Harrison
C. Hudson
Margaret Issitt

Sophie Kenyon
Emily Larnder
Paul Laybourn
Vikki Lea
Harlen Leonard
Emma Lillie
Hannah Marklew
John McColgar
B. McCormick
Kris McGill
Nicky Mitchell
Amanda Morris
William Morriss
Abigail Munden
Stuart Munro
Jeannie Ogilvie
Robert Otley

Neesha Rawal
Heather Richardson
Laura Ridley
C. Robinson
Debbie Robson
Jenny Rowlands
Scott Shields
Matthew Shipman
Penny Smith
Rosalyn Smith
Tom Starey
Danielle Step
Adam Sutton
Charlotte Tew
Vikky Ward
Rebecca Waring
Andrew Winfield

Become a Consultant!

Would you like to give us feedback on our titles before they are published? Contact us at the address below – we'd love to hear from you!

E-mail: info@barringtonstoke.co.uk
Website: www.barringtonstoke.co.uk